Black Man, Where Art Thou?

by

Rev. Dr. Perry Simmons, Jr.

Orman Press
Lithonia, Georgia

Black Man, Where Art Thou?

by
Rev. Dr. Perry Simmons, Jr.

Copyright © 2004
Rev. Dr. Perry Simmons, Jr.

ISBN: 1-891773-58-5

Scripture quotations are taken from THE HOLY BIBLE, *King James Version*, or are the author's paraphrase of that version.

Printed in the United States of America

10 9 8 7 6 5 4 3 2

Publishing Services Provided By
Orman Press, Inc.
Lithonia, Georgia

— Dedication —

I would like to dedicate this book to my father, the late Rev. Perry Simmons, Sr. of Cairo, Georgia. My father was a man who believed in taking care of his family. He was always there for us. He did not make a whole lot of money, but we never went hungry. We were never cold in the winter and all of us who wanted to go to college went. He made the ultimate sacrifice to see that we were all educated.

My father was one of the best preachers that God has ever called into the gospel ministry. Many souls are saved today because my father *"was not ashamed of the gospel of Christ, for it is the power of God unto salvation" (Romans 1:16)*.

Thank you, Dad, for being there and being my friend.

— Acknowledgements —

I would like to acknowledge and thank all of the people who provided help, insight, material, encouragement and input into this book.

Deacon Stanley Weaks, a deacon at the Abyssinian Baptist Church, 224 West Kinney Street, Newark, New Jersey, where I have served as pastor since June 20, 1982. This book was inspired by a Men's Day message that Deacon Weaks brought to the men of Abyssinian in April 2000. Deacon Weaks also contributed to the Introduction of this book.

My father, the late **Rev. Perry Simmons, Sr.**, who pastored the St. Matthew Baptist Church, Donaldsonville, Georgia; the Second Saint James Baptist Church, Bainbridge, Georgia; and the Antioch Baptist Church, Camilla, Georgia. My father was always there for his wife and eleven children. We always felt secure because he was present to provide for us and to protect us.

My mother, **Pinkie Simmons,** of Cairo, Georgia. She is a strong woman who is always there to give direction to my brothers, sisters and me. My mother is the woman God had in mind when He described a good mother.

My late grandparents, **Elder William Henry Norwood**, Past Moderator of the Primitive Baptist Church; and **Annier Norwood**, who passed away in February 2000. Grandma Annier was a mother to the whole village of Cairo, Georgia. I miss her dearly.

Rhondea Williams, who helped with the editing of this book.

My loving and devoted wife, **Emma Pinckney Simmons**, who when I was sick in 2002, became my personal nurse and lovingly nurtured me back to good health.

Finally, I thank the **members of the Abyssinian Baptist Church in Newark, New Jersey**, for their support of me as their pastor and servant.

— Table of Contents —

Black Man, Where Art Thou?

This book is necessary because I am very concerned about my black brothers and their absence from their families, society and the church. It concerns me that too many of our black families are headed by women because the black man is absent. Our sons are looking beyond the home for role models because the black man is missing.

I am disturbed that there are more than 1.3 million black men who have lost their right to vote because they are either in prison or on parole. That is enough votes to sway the next election for the president of the United States.

I am alarmed that there are more women in seminaries than there are men, which means that our churches will be headed more and more by women if this trend does not change. Although more men are coming back to church, I feel that we should put forth an all out effort to evangelize lost men, especially black men.

I hope and pray that every black man in particular, and every man in general, will read this book and decide to make Jesus his Lord, and answer the question: "**Black man, where art thou?**" by saying, "Here am I, Lord. Send me. I'll go."

And the eyes of them both were opened, and they knew that they were naked; and they sewed fig leaves together, and made themselves aprons. And they heard the voice of the LORD God walking in the garden in the cool of the day: and Adam and his wife hid themselves from the presence of the LORD God amongst the trees of the garden. And the LORD God called unto Adam, and said unto him, Where art thou? And he said, I heard thy voice in the garden, and I was afraid, because I was naked; and I hid myself. And he said, Who told thee that thou wast naked? Hast thou eaten of the tree, whereof I commanded thee that thou shouldest not eat? And the man said, The woman whom thou gavest to be with me, she gave me of the tree, and I did eat. And the LORD God said unto the woman, What is this that thou hast done? And the woman said, The serpent beguiled me, and I did eat (Genesis 3:7–13).

INTRODUCTION

Black Man, Where Art Thou?

— Genesis 3:7–13 —

T here was a time when there was no evil and no sin upon the earth, a time when the whole world was perfect and clothed in perfection. But the day came when sin entered the world. We see in Genesis 3:1–7 that consequences began to occur immediately when sin entered the world. The first consequence of sin was man's tragic fall from perfection. Sin crushed and devastated Adam and Eve's image of themselves. Genesis 3:7–13 shows us five traits of low self image that are consequences of sin.

Low Self-Esteem Trait 1:

The sense of being naked, imperfect, corruptible and short of God's righteousness (Gen. 3:7).

As soon as Adam and Eve sinned, their eyes were opened and they immediately knew something: they were stark naked. This probably means two things. First, the clothing of perfection and innocence was stripped away. Note the statement, *"Their eyes were opened and they knew that they were naked"* (Genesis 3:7). This could not mean their physical eyes, for the eyes of their body had been opened since their creation. Therefore, it must mean the eyes of their heart, mind and conscience. Before they sinned, Adam and Eve were morally perfect and innocent, sinless and righteous. When they sinned, a radical change took place within their hearts and minds. They immediately knew that something was wrong. They no longer felt perfect and innocent, sinless and righteous. Within their hearts and minds they sensed guilt and shame. They knew beyond all question that they had done wrong. They knew both good and evil, for they had eaten the fruit of evil. They had turned away from God, disobeyed His Word and rebelled against Him. The consequences of sin had taken effect—sin had stripped them naked. They were now imperfect, guilty of rebelling against God, sinful and unrighteous.

Secondly, the clothing of God's glory and righteousness was stripped away. Remember, Adam was created in the image and likeness of God. The Bible tells us that God is light (I John 1:5) and that God covers Himself with light as with a garment (Psalm 104:2). God's glory is so brilliant and full of so much splendor that it has stricken a terrifying fear in men when they have witnessed it. An example is the shepherds at the birth of Christ (Luke 2:9–10). Remember also the transfiguration of Christ; the glory of God changed the whole countenance of Christ. His face shone like the sun and His clothes became as white as light itself (Matthew 17:2). Just imagine what the image and likeness of God is

4

like in His glory, in the brilliance and splendor of the light of His presence.

My point is this: Adam and Eve were created in the image and likeness of God. This was bound to include, at least to some degree, some of the glory and righteousness of God's being. In their perfect bodies and within their perfect environment (the Garden of Eden), some of God's glory and righteousness must have dwelt within and shone out of their bodies. The image and likeness of God must have covered and clothed Adam and Eve in their perfect state of being. But note what happened when they sinned—they immediately became naked. They lost the covering of God's glory and righteousness. They had turned away from God, rejected His life, the way of perfection, glory, and righteousness. Sin caused a radical change within their bodies and countenance, a change so radical that the glory, light and righteousness of God was stripped away from them. Their bodies were radically changed from perfect to imperfect, from incorrupt to corruptible, from glorious to dishonorable, from power-filled to weak. Their bodies changed from a spiritual body to a natural body.

Low Self-Esteem Trait 2:

An attempt to cover their sin and shame (Gen. 3:7).

The person who sins always tries to hide and cover his sin to keep others from finding out. Why? Because of shame. He is ashamed of his sin and failure so he does not want people to know about it. This was true of Adam and Eve. When they partook of the forbidden fruit, they immediately felt shame and guilt. Before they sinned, they felt no shame whatsoever, but now they felt deep intense shame. We see and experience so much sin and shame that we become hardened and immune to both, but not Adam and Eve. They had never seen or experienced wrong doing. This was the first sin and shame ever seen or experienced by man. The shame they felt must have been the most intense and terrifying shame imaginable. This is what made them cover themselves with aprons made of fig leaves. They were trying to cover the shame and guilt they were feeling.

Why did they cover only their sexual organs? There are at least two reasons. Firstly, it was the only part of the body that fig leaves could reasonably cover. A person's movement would be greatly hindered if leaves were wrapped around his legs, shoulders, and arms. To cover these parts of the body with an apron of fig leaves would not make sense. Secondly, according to H.C. Leupold, the great Lutheran expositor, they covered that part of the body from which human nature comes. They covered the reproductive organs because they instinctively felt that human life was now contaminated by sin. It was from that part of the body that fallen mankind was now to be born. Therefore, Adam and Eve instinctively covered that which best represented the fallen, corrupt nature of man.

Low Self-Esteem Trait 3:

Running away and hiding from God (Genesis 3:8).

There are two significant facts in this point. Firstly, it was apparently the habit of God to appear to Adam and Eve and share with them in fellowship and communion. Remember, fellowship was one of the primary reasons God created man. Therefore, God's *walking in the garden in the cool of the day* was to be expected. It was His habit, His custom, to come to Adam and Eve and fellowship with them.

Secondly, Adam and Eve ran away and hid themselves from God. What an abrupt change! They had often heard God walking in the garden and calling out to them. Their hearts had always leaped with joy, excitement and great expectation when they heard the sound of His strong, yet tender and welcoming voice. They had always run to meet Him, just as a child runs to meet his father who has been away for awhile, but something terrible had happened since God's last visit. Adam and Eve had turned away from God. They had disobeyed God. They had rebelled against God. They had decided to do what they wanted instead of what God wanted. Adam and Eve had chosen to follow self and Satan instead of following God. The result of their disobedience was catastrophic: their whole being, both inwardly and outwardly, spiritually and physically was marred and corrupted. They were stripped naked. They were no longer perfect and innocent. They no longer possessed the glow of God's glory, light and righteousness. They were now separated, cut off and alienated from God. This is why Adam and Eve fled and tried to hide themselves from God. They did not want to face God. They did not want to face the fact of their sin. They did not want to give an account for their behavior. They did not want to suffer the judgment and punishment. Simply put, they did not want to face the consequences of their sins. God had made Himself clear: if you partake of the forbidden fruit, you shall die.

Man still tries to run away and hide from God by:

- refusing to sit under the preaching of God's Word.
- never seeking God.
- never reading and studying the Bible.
- never praying.
- refusing to allow loved ones and neighbors to talk to him about God.
- denying the existence of God.
- ignoring and neglecting God.
- pushing thoughts about God out of his mind.
- denying there is such a thing as sin, guilt or conscience.
- stressing the physical world of science, technology, philosophy and psychology.
- minimizing or denying the spiritual world.

Man tries to hide behind everything imaginable to keep from facing God. But David said in Psalm 139:7–12:

> *Whither shall I go from thy spirit? or whither shall I flee from thy presence? If I ascend up into heaven, thou art there: if I make my bed*

in hell, behold, thou art there. If I take the wings of the morning, and dwell in the uttermost parts of the sea; Even there shall thy hand lead me, and thy right hand shall hold me. If I say, Surely the darkness shall cover me; even the night shall be light about me. Yea, the darkness hideth not from thee; but the night shineth as the day: the darkness and the light are both alike to thee.

In Genesis 3:9, God asked Adam a question: "Adam, where art thou?" This is a startling question because God knew exactly where Adam was. God knows everything. What, then, was God doing? This is the call of the seeking Savior. God's heart had been broken by Adam's sin. In His infinite knowledge, God saw all the ages, centuries, decades, years and days of sin and shame that lay ahead for fallen man. God saw acts of lying, stealing, cheating, killing, wars, maiming and immorality. God saw all the broken homes and lives, all the pain and hurt, all the suffering that would be borne by men, women and children through the days and centuries of history. God saw the great price He would have to pay to complete His purpose upon earth. He saw that He would have to give His Son to pay the penalty for man's sin. *"For the son of man is come to seek and to save that which was lost" (Luke 19:10).*

God knew exactly where Adam was. The question, *"Adam, where art thou?"* was not for God's information; it was to stir Adam to think about where he was. It was the call of godly conviction. Adam was running away and hiding from God. God was calling out to Adam in order to arouse conviction within him. Adam needed to think about what he was doing. He was running away and hiding from the only person who could reconcile and help him; the only person who could correct, rectify and salvage the situation; the only person who could give him guidance, direction, peace, security, love, joy, hope and life upon this earth. Jesus, the only person who could save, said in John 16:8, *"And when he (the Holy Spirit) is come, he will reprove the world of sin, and of righteousness, and of judgment."*

Adam's sin was a terrible sin against God. In fact, Adam's sin was the same terrible sin that we commit against God. Adam did the same terrible thing that we do when we sin. He turned away from God, the only person who could tell him how to escape the judgment of death that was to soon fall upon him and snatch him from this world. He disobeyed God. He rebelled against God. He refused to live for God and do what God commanded. Rebellion is the most violent act a person can commit against God. When God created Adam, He told Adam that the penalty for sin was death. Therefore, God's call to Adam was a call to justice, a summons to judgment. Adam was to appear before the court of God and face the sentence of death because he had to bear the judgment of his rebellion and insurrection against God.

Men, you may try to run away and hide from God. You may deny, ignore and neglect God, but the day is coming when God will call you before His court of justice, and every one of you will be judged. You will be judged because you turned away from God, because you disobeyed God and because you rebelled against God. Hebrews 9:27 says *"And as it is appointed unto men once to die, but after this the judgment."*

Low Self-Esteem Trait 4:

Disturbed relationships and severe divisions caused by sin (Genesis 3:10–13).

Sin disturbs a man's relationship with God and causes division between him and God. This was seen when Adam ran away and hid from God. The perfect relationship he had known with God no longer existed. He had fellowshipped face-to-face with God, but not now. Adam now feared God. He feared God because he was naked. He was no longer perfect and innocent. He was no longer full of God's glory and righteousness. He was no longer in the image and likeness of God. Adam was now totally different from God. A wall of disturbed feelings and division separated Adam from God. Adam was a sinner. God was perfect, whole, glorious and righteous. When Adam faced God, he would have to bear the penalty and judgment for sin, causing a great division in his relationship with God. This is why Adam feared God.

Sin has caused a great gulf, and a terrifying division between us and God. Our relationship with God has been so disturbed by sin that we are doomed unless we cast ourselves totally upon God, and commit all we are and have to follow Him.

According to verses 11 through 13, sin disturbs man's relationship with others and causes severe division. God asked Adam two questions: *"Who told you that you were naked?"* and *"Have you eaten the forbidden fruit?"* Note three facts here in Adam's response. Firstly, Adam blamed Eve. He said, *"The woman gave me the fruit."* Secondly, he blamed God. He said, *"The woman **you** gave to be with me enticed me to eat of the forbidden fruit."* Thirdly, Eve blamed the serpent. She said, *"The serpent deceived me."* Eve did not accept blame for her sin any more than Adam (did). Eve was really saying that God should have kept the devil from tempting her and causing her to sin.

Black men, each of us must give an account for our own sins. We must repent of our sins. God has provided salvation and eternal life for us, but we must be honest and quit blaming others. We must do just what the Scripture says: *"Repent ye: for the kingdom of heaven is at hand"* *(Matthew 3:2).*

Black man, where art thou?

CHAPTER ONE

Men Missing In Action

— II Timothy 4:10 —

"For Demas hath forsaken me, having loved this present world, and is departed unto Thessalonica; Crescens to Galatia, Titus unto Dalmatia."

One of the most serious problems during war is accounting for persons who disappear from the battlefield. In addition to all the other distasteful elements connected to the Vietnam war, there is still the question of what happened to the more than 2,800 men who are unaccounted for. They were once listed as members of the armed forces of the United States of America. They were committed to the task of liberating millions of impoverished people in the third world from communist domination. They were well-trained and well-equipped for the task to which they had been assigned, but somehow in the heat of the battle, they disappeared. We do not know if they were killed, captured or defected, asking for political asylum in the enemy's camp. All we know is that they are listed as "Missing in Action."

The friends and relatives of people who are missing in action experience a perpetual nightmare of emotional suffering—one of waiting, wishing, yearning, longing and hoping. Wives and sweethearts of MIAs are left in limbo. On the one hand, they do not want to give up on the relationship they had in the past as long as there is a ray of hope left; although the chances of their husbands and potential husbands being alive and returning home are slim. On the other hand, they do not want to miss out on someone with whom they could have a meaningful relationship for the future. So the nightmare continues. They do not know what to do. Their lives are filled with unanswered questions about their husbands and sweethearts' return, and unsolved problems because they were once very close to someone who is now Missing in Action.

Missing persons is not just a dilemma of war. One of the growing problems in our civilian society is an ever-increasing number of persons whose whereabouts are unknown. There are television programs designed to locate missing persons. The situation has become so grave that parents are afraid to let their small children play in the yard unless they are there to watch them.

The thing that disturbs me most about this phenomenon is that while there is a growing concern about missing persons in the military and in the secular society, the Christian community shows little concern for those who have disappeared from the battlefield of Christian warfare. We do not have to do any research to determine that many of our church members, especially our men, are Missing in Action. All we have to do is just look around and see the empty seats that should be filled with men. These empty seats tells us that many of those who signed up to be soldiers in God's army are now spiritually Missing in Action.

There is a difference between military MIAs and spiritual MIAs. We do not know if the military MIAs are dead or alive, but their families and loved ones still care about them. We know that those who are spiritually Missing in Action are physically alive, but spiritually dead. They are still on this side of the grave, but they are Missing in Action. They have either been captured by Satan or have voluntarily defected to his camp and asked for spiritual asylum.

Some of them were once very active. Some of them held high offices and prestigious positions in the church. Some used to sing in the choir and serve in the ushers ministry. Some served in the missionary, deacon and trustee ministries. Some attended prayer meetings and Bible study classes. Some were once full of the Holy Ghost and spiritual enthusiasm, but now when we look around, we have to say that they are Missing in Action. We still carry their names on the church roll, but they never show their faces. A few are "C.M.E." members who only come three days a year— Christmas, Mother's Day and Easter. Because we have twice as many names on the roll as we have in attendance on Sunday morning, we can conclude that many of our men are Missing in Action.

Just as the families of the military MIAs are concerned about the fate of their loved ones, we ought to be just as concerned about the fate and the whereabouts of our missing men. Just as the U.S. government and family members are making trips to Southeast Asia looking for their MIAs, we ought to be searching our communities, making telephone calls and knocking on doors to find our missing men. Their return should be the main item on our agenda.

The parable of the lost sheep dramatizes the concern that we should have over just one missing man. The recovery of that lost one became the shepherd's top priority and he didn't give up until he had found him. This challenges me as a minister of the gospel and as the under-shepherd of the flock of the Abyssinian Baptist Church. I realize that I have a responsibility to seek the whereabouts of those who are Missing in Action. Not only should I be concerned about them, but they should be your concern also.

Sometimes, the sheep that remain in the fold can do a better job finding lost sheep than the shepherd because sheep know where other sheep hang out. Sometimes missing sheep will reveal their whereabouts to another sheep quicker than they will to the shepherd. So it is our joint responsibility to show concern for the sheep that have strayed away from the fold.

Sometimes all they need to know is that somebody cares and that they will be welcomed when they return to the fold. However, a lot of sheep stay away from the fold because they are apathetic. They have a "don't care" attitude. In far too many instances, our attitude toward lost sheep is summarized in the nursery rhyme entitled "Little Bo-Peep."

Little Bo-Peep has lost her sheep,
And can't tell where to find them.
Leave them alone,
And they'll come home,
Wagging their tails behind them.

Many of us have the same attitude concerning those who are Missing in Action. We have lost our men and we don't know where to find them. So we will just leave them alone and hope they will come home wagging their tails behind them.

In II Timothy 4:10, we have an account of a young man, Demas, who got lost on the battlefield of Christian warfare and was subsequently listed as Missing in Action. At one time Demas was a companion of the Apostle Paul. Many church goers have never heard of Demas, for his name is mentioned only three times in the Bible. In his letters to the Colossians and Philemon, Paul mentioned that Demas was with him, but in II Timothy 4:10, Paul said that *"Demas has forsaken me."*

We know three things about Demas. Firstly, we know for a while he was with Paul. He was a soldier in God's army. He was committed to the cause of Christ. Secondly, we know that he left Paul and went AWOL. He was "absent without leave." He became a deserter from the Christian army.

When Paul looked around for him, he was nowhere to be found. Indeed he was Missing in Action. Thirdly, we know that, according to Paul, he left *"because he loved this present world more than he loved the cause of Christ."*

Think about that my friends. We know three things about Demas and two of them are bad. The one good thing that we know is that he joined the church, became a follower of Christ and was a companion of Paul. The two bad things that we know about him are that he quit the church, and the reason he quit was because he loved this present world more than he loved the cause of Christ. I don't have to tell you that's bad.

As a minister and a pastor, I experience this type of thing all the time. I get letters from various companies and agencies where my members are seeking employment, and in many instances they are just like Demas. I only know three things about them and two of them are bad. All I know is that they joined the church, they quit the church, and the reason they quit the church was because they loved worldly pleasure more than they loved Jesus Christ. I must admit that I do not always tell the whole truth on reference letters. I sometimes deviate from the truth to help my members get jobs. Sometimes I put "excellent" labels on "mediocre" and "inferior" products. I give recommendations on faith. When I write good things about people who are Missing in Action, I just believe and hope that they are going to come back and do better.

Let us continue to look at Demas, this young man who was listed as Missing in Action. Since he went to Thessalonica when he left Paul, it is reasonable to assume that this was his home. It is quite possible that while Paul was there conducting an evangelistic campaign, Demas was converted. No doubt Paul told him about his Damascus road experience and he was so excited until he joined the church. Maybe Paul did not take the time to tell him about the pitfalls that we encounter on this Christian journey. Maybe Paul only told him about the "milk and honey" side of Christianity. Maybe he did not mention that sometimes we have to drink the cup of sorrow. But Paul's sermon was so appealing that when he concluded and opened the doors of the church, Demas jumped up out of his seat, ran down the aisle and gave him his hand. Later, he was one of the first to sign up to serve on the foreign mission.

So when Paul left on his missionary journey, Demas was with him as an active member of Paul's team. He was a dedicated soldier in the Christian army. He stayed with Paul and worked diligently as long as things were going well, but when they got to Rome and Paul went on trial before a merciless emperor, Demas began to lose some of his enthusiasm. In some of the towns where Paul preached, the people were friendly and the love offerings were generous, but when they got to Rome, Paul was imprisoned because it was against Roman law to be a Christian.

So as Demas began to think about the danger he was facing, the devil began to tell him about the pleasures of the world he was missing. No doubt Satan reminded Demas about all of the swinging night clubs he used to go to and about all of the beautiful women he used to date. He probably told him that he was too young to be wasting his life with this old preacher who was about to get his head chopped off. "You ought to go back home and have yourself some fun while you are still young. Go back home and get yourself a good job, make yourself some good money and have yourself a good time."

The more Demas thought about this, the more his fleshly desires began to take over. The more he listened to Satan, the more his appetite grew for worldly pleasures. Finally, he made up his mind to quit the Christian army and go back into the world. When Paul began to look around for Demas, he was nowhere to be found. So Paul took out his list of companions and beside Demas' name he wrote, Missing in Action. No, Demas was not killed in battle; he just loved his worldly pleasures. He was not captured by the enemy; he just couldn't conquer his thirst for sin. He defected and took up residence in Satan's camp. He asked for and got spiritual asylum from Satan.

Many so-called Christian men have become weak just like Demas. When the church needs them, they are Missing in Action. When they are needed "to do God's will," they are out "doing their own thing." When they need to be "catching men," they are out on the banks "catching fish." When they ought to be "singing and praying," they are somewhere "swinging and swaying." When they need to be "working in a church ministry," they are "sitting in a night club." When they ought to be "witnessing," they are somewhere "gossiping." When they ought to be in church saying "amen," they are at home "relaxing in their paneled dens." When they ought to be "kneeling at the altar," they are out there "sitting at the bar." When they ought to be in church "clapping their hands and patting their feet," they are out "somewhere walking the streets." When they ought to be in the church "shouting hallelujah," they are out somewhere "getting their groove on." When they ought to be in church "partaking of the bread and wine," they are out on Saturday night partaking of the "whiskey and shine." They are Missing in Action.

In his book, *Making a Missionary Church*, Stacy Warburton wrote, "Essentially, the church has many responsibilities but only one mission, and that is to evangelize and disciple all nations." I would like to narrow Warburton's statement a little and say that the church's mission is to evangelize and disciple lost men.

The church must issue a wake-up call to African-American men and work to alter the black man's thinking to believe that things can change. Our men need to know that Satan is the real power behind the evil that plagues our race. The Apostle Paul said, *"For we wrestle not against flesh and blood, but against principalities, against powers, against the rulers of the darkness of this world, against spiritual wickedness in high places" (Ephesians 6:12).*

Black men, you can make a difference; however, you must wake up and reclaim your heritage in Christ, return to biblical principles and teachings and restore the spirit of achievement. Black men must turn "I can't" into "Yes, I can." They must turn "I don't know" into "I'm learning." They must turn "give me" into "What do you need me to give?"

Yet, we cannot make a difference if we are Misssing in Action. I don't know about you, but when my Commander in Chief comes around and calls the roll, I want to be on the job. I do not want to be Missing in Action when He comes back for His church. I want to be somewhere listening for my name. And in order for me to answer him when He calls me, I will have to stay on the battlefield. As the old spiritual says, "I promised him that I would serve him till I die, I am on the battlefield for my lord."

Black men, we have to stay on the battlefield, because one of these days, Jesus is coming back again. Don't let Him catch you with your work undone.

Black man, where are you?
Why are you missing in action?

CHAPTER TWO

Unkempt Vineyards

— Song of Solomon 1:5–6 —

"I am black, but comely, O ye daughters of Jerusalem, as the tents of Kedar, as the curtains of Solomon. Look not upon me, because I am black, because the sun hath looked upon me: my mother's children were angry with me; they made me the keeper of the vineyards; but mine own vineyard have I not kept."

Song of Solomon 1:5–6 seems to be dealing with Christ and His love for the church. It tells us that the church has some defects, but the love of Christ covers all defects of the church. The bride in the text feels unworthy because when she compares her complexion to that of the daughters of Jerusalem or concubines, she found that she was much darker than they. So, lest the other women in Solomon's harem should look down on her because of her complexion, she cried out, *"I am black but comely, O ye daughters of Jerusalem, as the tents of Kedar, as the curtains of Solomon."* She was saying, "I am black, but I am good looking." She said she was like the tents of Kedar, which were made of hides from goats with black hair. However, she also likened herself to the magnificent curtains of Solomon's palace. In an effort to explain her dark complexion, she said in verse 6:

> *Look not upon me, because I am black, because the sun hath looked upon me; they made me keeper of the vineyards; but my own vineyard have I not kept.*

She blamed her condition upon her mother's children, who, evidently were her stepbrothers and sisters. She said, *"My mother's children were angry with me; they made me keeper of the vineyards."* The result was that she could not care for her own personal appearance as the other girls could.

A vineyard is a place with grapevines. It can also be a field of activity, especially religious work. It is in this vein that I would like to deal with "unkempt vineyards."

Our Economic Vineyards

The black man has been keeping the economic vineyard of white America, but has not kept his own vineyard. We are still spending all of our money everywhere, but in our own community.

Blacks generate more than $200 billion into the economy. We spend $30 billion for food, $10 billion for cars, $20 billion for clothes, $10 billion for recreation, $35 billion for housing, and we spend it all in the white community. Our food money is spent at A&P, Food Town, Shoprite, Piggly Wiggly, Morrison's, Piccadilly's, Kentucky Fried Chicken,

McDonald's, Wendy's, Popeye's, Burger King, etc. Our money for cars goes to white-owned dealerships. Our money for clothes goes to Macy's, Lord and Taylor, The Gap, Annie Sez, Hit or Miss, Victoria's Secret, etc.

We see a decline in black businesses across America because the black man has not kept his own economic vineyard. Because most of our black recording artists have turned to white record companies, many of our black record labels have declined or even gone out of business. Many black-owned radio stations have gone under because of a lack of advertising dollars from major white corporations that we help to build through our financial support of their products. We have few black businesses to employ young black men and women or nurture those who want to start their own businesses. Many of our black-owned banks do not have the resources to finance our business enterprises because we do not invest in our own banks, and neither do whites.

We need to form corporations in our communities. We need black-owned automobile dealerships, supermarkets, hotels and restaurants. Yes, the black man has been keeping the white man's economic vineyards, but he has not kept his own. If we expect to protect the gains we have made in this country, we must start keeping our own economic vineyard.

Our Political Vineyard

We have not kept our political vineyard. Politics is the art and science of government. To be good, productive citizens, we must be active participants in our government. We must register to vote and then vote in every election. We do not have enough representation in our state and national congresses. Following Reconstruction, Mississippi had two black U.S. senators: Hiram R. Revels and Blanche K. Bruce. Today, there are no black senators from Mississippi. In 1982, Robert Clark, a black man lost the Second Congressional District in Mississippi because blacks joined with white Republicans to defeat him. We lost a chance to have a black President in Rev. Jessie Jackson. We did not believe that he could win so many of us voted for his opponent or did not bother to vote at all. We remove ourselves from the decision-making process in America when we choose not to partici-pate in the electoral process. Our political vineyard is unkempt simply because we do not vote.

Our Church Vineyard

As black Christians, we have not kept the vineyard of our church. Christ instituted the church as a vital part of God's divine plan for man. The church originated in and through Jesus Christ. Christ established His church to carry forward His message of salvation after His earthly ministry was completed.

One day, He stopped on the coast of Caesarea Philippi and asked His disciples, *"Whom do men say that I, the Son of man, am?" (Matthew 16:13).* They responded by saying, *"Some say that thou art John the Baptist, Elias, Jeremias, or one of the other prophets" (Matthew 16:14).* He then turned to them and asked, *"But whom say ye that I am?"* *(Matthew 16:15).*

> *And Simon Peter answered and said, 'Thou are the Christ, the son of the living God.' And Jesus answered and said unto him, Blessed are thou Simon Bar-jona, for flesh and blood hath not revealed it unto thee, but my father which is in heaven. And I say also unto thee, that thou art Peter and upon this rock I will build my church; and the gates of hell shall not prevail against it. And I will give you the keys to the kingdom of heaven: and whatsoever thou shalt bind on earth shall be bound in heaven: and whatsoever thou shalt loose on earth shall be loosed in heaven (Matthew 16:16–19).*

We have not kept the vineyard of our church attendance. As Christians, we are to attend church.

> *Not forsaking the assembling of ourselves together, as the manner of some is; but exhorting one another and so much the more, as ye see the day approaching (Hebrews 10:25).*

We go to our jobs and our fraternity and sorority meetings, but we neglect to go to the house of God. There has been a great exodus from the black church. Many have just stopped coming to church altogether, especially our black men. Many of them do not seem to find what they are looking for in the church anymore so they are turning to the Nation of Islam and other organizations.

Our vineyard of church support is unkempt. If we love God, then we will support His cause.

> *Even from the days of your fathers ye are gone away from my ordinances, and have not kept them. Return unto me and I will return unto you, saith the Lord of hosts. But ye said, Wherein shall we return? Will a man rob God? Yet ye have robbed me. But ye say, wherein have we robbed thee? In tithes and offerings. Ye are cursed with a curse: for ye have robbed me, even this whole nation. Bring ye all the tithes into the storehouse, that there may be meat in mine house, and prove me now herewith, saith the Lord of hosts, if I will not open you the windows of heaven, and pour you out a blessing, that there shall not be room enough to receive it (Malachi 3:7–10).*

One's use of money is often a barometer of his spirituality. If you want to know how much a man loves God, look at his checkbook. If a man truly loves God, he will pay his tithe and he will pay it first before any other bill.

If a man loves God, he will also work in God's ministry. Many people look upon the church as a group of people that meets once a week or more. Some view it as a good hangout or a way to establish contacts in the community. But God looks at the church differently. God ordained the church to give the gospel to the world. Christ said:

> *The Spirit of the Lord is upon me, because he hath anointed me to preach the gospel to the poor; he hath sent me to heal the broken-hearted, to preach deliverance to the captives, and recovering of sight to the blind, to set at liberty them that are bruised, to preach the acceptable year of the Lord (Luke 4:18–19).*

That means that every church is a missionary organization and all the world is its field. The black church needs workers to fulfill Christ's mission of sharing the gospel and ministering to people who are lost, suffering and bound by sin. Our vineyard of church support is unkempt because we do not participate in the mission of the church.

Another vineyard that is unkempt is the one of prayer.

> *If my people, which are called by my name, shall humble themselves, and pray, and seek my face, and turn from their wicked ways; then will I hear from heaven, and will forgive their sin, and will heal their land (II Chronicles 7:14).*

The black man in America used to sing, "Every time I feel the spirit moving in my heart, I must pray," but today he does not take time to pray. The habit of prayer should be well cultivated because there is power in prayer.

Joshua prayed and the sun stood still (Joshua 10:12–13). Gideon prayed for a fleece wet with dew as a sign that God would save Israel by his hand, and the next morning Gideon wrung a bowl full of water from the fleece (Judges 6:36–40). Hannah prayed and God gave her a son (I Samuel 1:11–20). David prayed and God gave him a clean heart (Psalm 51:10). Elijah prayed on Mount Carmel and fire came down from heaven (2 Kings 1:9–10). Hezekiah prayed and God added fifteen years to his life (Isaiah 38:1–6). Daniel prayed and God delivered him in the lion's den (Daniel 6:16–23). The Hebrew boys prayed and God delivered them in the fiery furnace (Daniel 3:14–30). Peter prayed for a lame man and the man began walking and leaping and praising God (Acts 3:1–8). Stephen prayed for his enemies as they stoned him and he slept peacefully into death (Acts 7:58–60). Paul prayed for instruction and God made him a chosen vessel to bear His name before the Gentiles, kings and children of Israel (Acts 9:6–15). Paul and Silas prayed when they were in jail in Philippi and the keeper of the jail and his whole house was saved (Acts 16:25–33).

When our forefathers needed help, they looked to the hills from whence cometh their help. They looked to Jesus, their bread in a starving land; their bridge over troubled water; their way out of no way; their doctor in a sick room; their lawyer in a courtroom. They looked to Jesus because they knew He was able to perform miracles in a desert place.

They looked to Jesus because He was the one who died on the cross, stayed in the grave for three days and rose early on Sunday morning with all power in His hand.

We can no longer afford to leave our vineyards unkempt. No one is going to do for our people what God has assigned us to do.

Black man, where are you?
Why are your vineyards unkempt?

"The crime that the white man has committed is that he taught the black man how to hate himself."
Malcom X

"The last bastion of white supremacy is in the black man's mind."
Nikki Giovanni

"If a person cannot change his mind, he cannot change anything."
George Bernard Shaw

"The problem with success is that it puts struggle to sleep."
Louis Farrakhan

"To be a Negro in America and to be relatively conscious is to be in a rage almost all of the time."
James Baldwin

"In a racist society, the normal person is racist."
Frantz Fanon

"If you make a man feel inferior, you do not have to compel him to accept inferior status, for he will seek it himself."
Carter G. Woodson

"The destruction of the black male is the biggest problem facing the black family."
Dr. Janice Hale

"Power corrupts and absolute power corrupts absolutely."
Lord Acton

"Nothing will be saved until souls are saved."
Fulton Sheen

CHAPTER THREE

The Plight of the Black Man in the New Millennium

— Proverbs 23:7 —

"For as he thinketh in his heart, so is he."

The 1990s left us with some very disturbing statistics. In the 1990s there were 1.3 million more marriageable black females than black males. Only 47 percent of all black families were married couples. More than 85 percent of all black youth lived in poverty. More than 42 percent of all black children lived in fatherless homes. Twenty-seven percent of all black children were being raised by high school dropouts. Black men accounted for more than 43 percent of the prison population.

One of the things that troubles me most today is that there appears to be a systematic genocide of young black males in America. Remember that Pharaoh tried to do the same thing when Moses was born. Herod tried to do the same thing when Jesus was born. And the same thing is happening to black men today. The power structure is always neurotically threatened by news of someone who can save and rescue the masses.

In a repressive society, the birth of anything liberating will be met with schemes of undermining treachery and murder. Wholesale conspiracy against young males of any race will devastate and cripple any people. However, no power structure, no matter how cunning or cruel, can permanently defeat the purpose of God for His people. Just as God intervened in the life of Moses and Jesus, He can do the same for the black man today.

There are two major problems that the young black man is facing in the new millennium. The first problem is that the young black male needs positive father figures and role models. One great poet said, "What one beholds, is what one becomes." Young black boys desperately need to see role models other than pimps, pushers, playboys, gang bangers, criminals and hustlers. Psychologists tell us that young black males will more readily imitate strong and caring black men who are around them than pimps and pushers.

The second problem is that because the black man feels powerless, he sees money and sex as power. For many black males, sexuality is an expression of power. In capitalistic America, money and manhood are inseparably joined. The more money a man makes, the more man he is. If a man is not making money, he's not a man. Because most black men do not make a lot of money, their manhood is severely questioned and crushed.

Enemies of the Black Male

Let me take the time to tell you some of the enemies of the black male. **The first enemy that the black man must conquer is self hatred.** Malcolm X said:

> The worst crime that the white man has committed is that he has taught the black man how to hate himself. For when a man hates himself, he will turn on himself; that's *suicide*. Then he will turn on others who look like himself; that's *fratricide*. This is why we have so much black-on-black crime. This is one of the major reasons why black men abuse black women. It is not so much that black men don't like black women, it is that black men hate themselves.

The second enemy that the black man must conquer is vicious competition among black females. It is unbelievable that so many black women are so immorally competitive that they will go after any woman's husband, boyfriend or fiancee. This immoral competitiveness has undermined God's plan for monogamy (one love) and produced playboys, divorces, broken homes and emotionally handicapped children.

The third enemy that the black man must conquer is his anti-church and anti-religion mentality. Black people who know their history clearly, know that God, the church, and the preacher have always undergirded and propelled black

people forward. Therefore, an anti-god or anti-church senti-
ment is anti-historical, counter productive and seriously
compromises the very foundation by which the black
community survives spiritually.

**The fourth enemy that the black man must conquer is
his acceptance of the white culture's values.** The cultural
values that are promoted on American television and in our
movies are those of the predominant white culture—money,
sex, status, cars, clothes, liquor and leisure. This costly
illusion makes it impossible for the black man to get his
head straight as he lives by the godless values of America.

**The fifth enemy that the black man must conquer is his
own selfishness.** The black male cannot afford to participate
in the egocentric "me generation." The black man must
never embrace the Darwinian theory of the survival of the
fittest because it is done at the expense of black unity and
community.

I am aware of the extreme sensitivity of the issue of black
men relating to white women. I am aware that people have
a God-given right to be with whomever they choose.
Nevertheless, several points must be made. William Grier,
Price Mashaw Cobbs, two black psychiatrists, and Frantz
Fanon, a Cuban psychiatrist, feel that the masses of black
men relate to white women in a compensatory fashion
involving the issues of *self-inflating power* and *self-deflating
revenge. Self-inflating power* describes the ego of some
black men that are inflated because they feel so privileged
and powerful to be involved with so valued a creature as the

white woman who has chosen him, even over white men. *Self-deflating revenge* involves black men of low esteem who relate to white women out of a sense of vengeance. By associating with white women, these black men are saying to the larger society, "You white men treated me like a dog, but this dog is messing with your white women."

We must also look at black women's reaction to black men dating white women. Most black women react to black men dating white women with anger. That is because the black man/white woman situation offends them on at least two levels. It offends them generally because no woman wants to feel that another woman has gotten the best of her. It offends them specifically because black women do not want white women having the best black men available.

Solutions for the Black Man in the New Millennium

Let me give you some solutions to the problems and plight of the black man in the new millennium. One solution is **education**. Black men must become literate. They must be able to read and write. They must be able to articulate their thoughts. Black men must be knowledgeable of their history and heritage. Every black man, regardless of his age, should read at least twenty books every year. Every black man needs training in how to be a responsible black man, husband and father.

Another solution to the plight and problem of the black man is **economics**. After being educated, black men must get jobs, and learn how to invest in their own people and community. Blacks spent more than $308 billion in the 1990s and more than $533 billion in the year 2000. That is a 73 percent increase in less than a decade. The problem is that we spend 95 percent of our income in non-black communities. We need to learn how and where to invest our money.

Another solution to the plight and problem of the black man is **social support**. Older positive black men must spend quality time coaching, directing and encouraging younger black men and boys. Positive black men must help single mothers with their sons. Black women must become more sensitive to black men. Our black women need to stop being competitive and start being a team mate.

But the most important solution to the plight and problem of the black man is **salvation**. More black men must become saved Christians. So that you are not confused on how to be saved, I think I need to tell you what Paul said in Romans 10:9–13:

> *That if thou shalt confess with thy mouth the Lord Jesus, and shalt believe in thine heart that God hath raised him from the dead, thou shalt be saved. For with the heart man believeth unto righteousness; and with the mouth confession is made unto salvation. For the scripture saith, Whosoever believeth on him shall not be ashamed. For there is no difference between the Jew and the Greek: for the same Lord over all is rich unto all that*

THE PLIGHT OF THE BLACK MAN IN THE NEW MILLENNIUM

*call upon him. For whosoever shall call upon
the name of the Lord shall be saved.*

Anyone can be saved because *"God so loved the world, that He gave His only begotten Son, that whosoever believeth in Him should not perish, but have everlasting life" (John 3:16).*

When the black man becomes saved, he can say as Paul did in Philippians 4:13, *"I can do all things through Christ which strengthens me."* When a black man becomes saved, he will be free of the bondage of this world because Jesus said in John 8:32, *"And ye shall know the truth, and the truth shall make you free."* When he becomes saved, he will fear no man because Paul said in II Timothy 1:7, *"For God hath not given us the spirit of fear; but of power, and of love, and of a sound mind."* When he becomes saved, he will never be forsaken because, David said in Psalm 27:10, *"When my father and my mother forsake me, then the Lord will take me up."* When he becomes saved, he will not have to worry when he feels weak and weary because, Isaiah said in Isaiah 40:31:

> *But they that wait upon the lord shall renew their strength; they shall mount up with wings as eagles; they shall run, and not be weary; and they shall walk, and not faint.*

The issues of the black man in the new millennium are great, but the God we serve is greater. The answer for the black man is in education, economics and social support;

but most importantly, the answer for the black man is salvation. When black men accept Christ as their savior and truly put Him on the throne of their lives, they will not have to worry about the new millennium because they will know:

> *The Lord is my shepherd, I shall not want. He maketh me to lie down in green pastures: He leadeth me beside the still waters. He restoreth my soul: He leadeth me in the paths of righteousness for His name's sake. Yea, though I walk through the valley of the shadow of death, I will fear no evil: for thou art with me; thy rod and thy staff they comfort me. Thou preparest a table before me in the presence of mine enemies: thou anointest my head with oil; my cup runneth over. Surely goodness and mercy shall follow me all the days of my life: and I will dwell in the house of the Lord for ever (Psalm 23).*

Black man, where are you?
Why are you not saved?

CHAPTER FOUR

The Role of the Black Man in His Family

— Jeremiah 5:1 —

"Run ye to and fro through the streets of Jerusalem, and see now, and know, and seek in the broad places thereof, if ye can find a man, if there be any that executeth judgment, that seeketh the truth; and I will pardon it."

A story is told of an eccentric Greek philosopher by the name of Diogenes who lived four centuries before the coming of Christ. He was seen one day at twelve o'clock noon running through the streets of Athens with a lighted lantern in his hand. When someone stopped him and inquired why he was going through the streets carrying a lighted lantern when the sun was at its highest peak, he responded, "I am seeking to find a man."

In other words, Diogenes was saying, "I am looking for a man." Perhaps you are asking, "How stupid and utterly naive can a person be? How emotionally disturbed and mentally depraved can a person become as to go down the street in the broad open daylight with a lantern saying that he's looking for a man?" Well, my name is not Diogenes. This is not the fourth century B.C. I am not in Athens,

Greece and I do not have a lighted lantern; yet, I am going up and down, to and fro, through the streets of America, trying to find a black man.

You have probably concluded that my elevator is not going to the top floor; that I am not playing with a full deck and that I am a prime candidate for some mental institution. Maybe you are thinking, "How could you possibly make such a statement? Finding a black man is not a difficult chore. All you have to do is go down on Martin Luther King Boulevard at any hour of the day, in any city or town in the United States, and you'll find a whole lot of black men. If you are still having some difficulty finding a black man, go down to your local county jail, state prison or federal prison and I am sure you will have no problem finding a black man in either of those places."

Remember now, I said I am looking for a black *man*; not a Negro male wearing a pair of pants; not a dark-skinned human being who is biologically equipped with male organs; not an ebony-hued soul brother who majors in slam dunking and exam flunking. We have a preponderance of those characters. I am not talking about some cool dude who plays music so loudly on his car radio that you can hear him coming three blocks away. I am not talking about some brown-skinned macho man who expresses his masculinity by carrying a blade and a rod, and terrorizing the neighborhood where he lives. Our communities are literally running over with guys who fit those descriptions. I am looking for a black *man*.

In the sixth century B.C., when Jeremiah was looking for a man in the streets of Jerusalem, he was searching for someone of the masculine gender who was honest, and who was seeking to know the truth. Those were the only two qualifications: he had to be honest and he had to be searching for truth. In the fourth century B.C., when Diogenes was running through the streets of Athens looking for a man, he was looking for one who was prudent, wise and had a contempt for the status quo.

Well, here I am in the twenty-first century, going through the streets of America looking for a black man who will meet just three requirements centered around his relationship with his family. As a matter of fact, these three qualifications tell us in clear and vivid terms exactly what the black man's role should be in his family. Each of these requirements begins with the letter "P" and as we discuss each one of them, I want you to join me in my search and see if you can assist me in finding a black man who fulfills these responsibilities for his family.

Present

The first "P" represents **presence**. The first role of the black man in his family is to be present. The absence of black males in the black family has caused, and is still causing, major social problems throughout this nation. God established the family when he placed Adam and Eve in the Garden of Eden. Do you realize that it was not until Adam was absent that the devil was able to come into the home and take over? The fact that Satan addressed Eve implies that Adam was not present. Satan did not visit until Adam was not at the home. Black families need the presence of a black man.

Too many black men have mastered the art of starting families, but have not mastered the art of maintaining a family. Black men have mastered the technique of making babies, but have not mastered the technique of taking care of the babies they make. Black men know how to start ball games. They are great pitchers during the first inning. They can really get a game started, but by the time the ninth inning rolls around and the catcher is ready to deliver, the pitcher is on another field starting a new ball game. We have to learn how to stay with the same team and finish the games we start.

I do not want to be overly critical. I realize that our conspicuous absence is not all our fault. I fully understand that our irresponsible attitudes are imbedded within us by 250 years of slavery when our foreparents were bought and sold like cattle. I am not unmindful of the fact that during those years of slavery some black men were chosen by their masters to be bucks, studs and breeders, and that they were carried to various plantations to act as baby-making machines. I am well aware of the fact that on some planta-tions, marriage between slaves was forbidden and that promiscuity was encouraged. I am also aware of the fact that on plantations where marriage was allowed, black men were dehumanized beyond description by seeing their wives being used against their will by the plantation owners and later giving birth to the master's child. Such incidents were not isolated events that happened every now and then. In some slave territories, it was a way of life. So, I realize that 250 years of sexual irresponsibility cannot be cured overnight. Yet, I also realize that slavery was officially abolished in 1863 and that our emancipation became a reality in 1865 when the Civil War ended. It seems to me that after 139 years of freedom, we should have learned how to accept our responsibility.

The black bucks, studs and breeders of today practice their dubious craft by choice, not by force. I realize that we got off to a bad start in this business of being present and serving as the head of the family, but after 139 years of freedom, it is time for us to practice social maturity. Black men need to be present in black families. The bedroom in black homes must become an every-night dwelling for black husbands, rather than a transient baby-making center for itinerant black lovers.

Black homes should be a place of nurturing for black children, a place in which the father is a permanent resident as opposed to an occasional visitor. The black man needs to be present in the black family. Black homes ought to be places where black children await with joyful anticipation the daily arrival of their father as he comes home from work, rather than places where they await the arrival of their mother's new boyfriend.

In case you didn't hear me the first time, let me say it again: Black men need to be present in the black family.

Provider

The second "P" as it relates to the role of the black men in his family represents **provider**. I am looking for a black man who is not just present, but one who provides for his family. The black man has the responsibility to be the bread winner. I realize that times have changed and that women are serving more and more in the labor force, and I have no problem with that. I understand that with prices as they are, two checks are better than one. However, the fact remains that whether the wife works or not, it is the husband's responsibility to provide for his family.

Once again, I realize that we got off to a bad start in the area of providing for our families. We were set free with nothing but what we had on our backs. Our forefathers were promised forty acres and a mule, but the Freedman Bureau reneged on that promise. Like you, I'm still waiting for my forty acres and my mule. I also realize that through the years, black men have been the last to be hired and the first to be fired, and that is still the practice today.

The sagging economy is not doing much to help us fulfill our role as providers in our homes. Yet, the fact remains that despite being short-changed by the government, despite being discriminated against on the labor front, and despite the sagging economy, our role as provider has not gone away. Therefore, we must have some initiative, some "get up and go." If we cannot find a job, we should create a job. I do not mean that we should sell crack cocaine.

Far too many of us are sitting around the house waiting on someone to bring us a job and lay it in our laps. If we are going to be providers, we must get out and work. I realize that unemployment in the black community is twice as high as it is in the white community. I realize that there is a shortage of work nationwide in fields where we are trained. I also realize that when you're on the bottom of the economic ladder, you can't afford to be choosy. We have to be willing to take whatever job comes along. It's bad to say it, but some of the people who are unemployed are jobless because they are too lazy and stubborn to work the jobs that are available.

If we are ever going to close the gap that exists between black families and the families of other races, we, as black men, must provide for our families. We can no longer be domestic dictators, household spectators, dining room instigators, refrigerator exterminators, living room agitators and bedroom manipulators. Instead we must be providers and facilitators. We must provide for our families' needs and ensure that our children are raised in godly homes to be godly, responsible adults.

Yes, I am looking for a black man who will provide for his family.

Protector

Finally, as we look at the role of black men in the black family, the third "P" represents protector. We must not only be present and provide for our families, but we must also protect them. Our wives and our children need the protection of a black male in the home. One of my fondest memories of my childhood is that of my father threatening to do bodily harm to a man who called my sister out of her name. I felt like a million dollars. My father had spoken and the insulting man had to shut up.

We need to protect our children from the menacing gangs in our communities. We need to protect them from the peddlers of pornographic materials. We need to protect them from the drug pushers who have taken over our neighborhoods. We need to protect our children from those who would destroy their souls with false doctrine. We need to protect our children from the lie that blacks are inferior and that the only certain areas in which they can succeed are basketball and rapping. We must protect our children from the lie that Willie Horton typifies all black American males. Yes, we must protect our children from every danger, gang, pusher, false doctrine, cult and lie that could destroy them.

Yes, I am looking for a black man who will protect his children. Don't you know that if they are going to be protected, we have to do it? We cannot expect anyone else to do for black families what black men were created to do. I know that we have some sympathizers and empathizers in other races, and we thank God for their concern and interest, but they do not have the same sensitivty that comes from having suffered because of our color.

In some instances, whites have experienced intellectual discrimination. As they tried to get certain jobs, they were told that they were not scholastically qualified. They were told that they did not have the proper degree, and that they did not meet the intellectual qualifications. However, this brought out the best in them and challenged them to go back to school and earn another degree. Then, when they came back, they were accepted.

Many other races have experienced economic discrimination. When they have been turned away because of their lack of finances, they worked harder. They became frugal and industrious, they accumulated a certain amount of wealth and when they went back to the place that had turned them down, they presented their financial portfolios and were accepted with open arms.

When we, the ebony-hued sons of former slaves applied for entrance into first class citizenship and the main stream of America, the doors were slammed in our faces. We presented our diplomas and our degrees. We brought our bank books and stock certificates, but the doors were slammed in our faces. We have known discrimination like no other group in America. That viper called racism is still raising its ugly head and spewing its venom all across this nation. Only those of us who have felt this pain and borne this burden can properly protect future generations from future harm.

We must be present. We must be providers. We must be protectors. This is the three dimensional role the black man must play in the black family.

I'm still looking for a black man. If there is anybody who qualifies; if there is a black man who is present, provides for his family and protects his family, we can shout now. When we find one, we cannot stop there. Like the shepherd, we must continue looking for the lost sheep. If you are a black man who is already present, providing and protecting, God needs you to help find another brother who is lost and bring him back to the fold.

As my mind runs back 2000 years, I see Jesus Christ carrying His cross up Calvary's rugged mountain. I see a black man standing on the road side. His name is Simon of Cyrene, and he is present at the very spot where Jesus falls down under the weight of the cross. Not only is black Simon present, but he provides the strength to carry the cross. He protects the blessed shoulders and sacred hands of Jesus from further damage. Black Simon realized that *"the government shall be upon his shoulders"* and that those precious hands must be nailed to the cross. So black Simon was present, he provided and he protected.

I think that these three Ps also apply to God. He is present. He is here right now. God is a provider. He supplies all of our needs according to His riches in glory. God is a protector. He protects his children from danger. God wants His black men to be like Him.

Black man, where art thou?

CHAPTER FIVE

Out of the Dark Past Comes a Bright Future

— I John 2:8 —

"Again, a new commandment I write unto you, which thing is true in him and in you: because the darkness is past, and the true light now shineth."

What is the dark? In history, it refers to a time when individual rights to create, think differently, or exercise free expression were severely limited. This period was known as the Dark Ages.

As a people, we have experienced a dark past. We have felt the sting of slavery, the bite of segregation and Jim Crow laws, and the crunch of a social system weighted against us. Our dark past reveals the history of a people who have struggled and survived the darkness of unfavorable times to reach a point where we can see the light of a bright and shining future. That future is guaranteed to us by a God upon whose promise we stand, in whom our faith is unwavering and because of whom our hope is unfaltering.

Let us look at the darkness of our past. Isaiah 5:20 suggests that darkness is associated with wickedness. He admonishes those who call good evil and evil good; who substitute darkness for light; who substitute bitter for sweet and sweet for bitter. In our historical experience, we have witnessed the truth of this text. We were often stripped of our ability to enjoy the fruits of our labor and instead beaten, forced to work for others and denied our civil rights.

Isaiah 42:7 suggests that darkness is a period of ignorance in which our eyes are closed and we are imprisoned by our lack of understanding. As a people, we know what it means to be kept from knowledge, and we have seen its results. The period of national ignorance was a dark period for us because without the tools to cultivate thinking, we were not apprised of even the possibility of our freedom.

First Corinthians 4:5 refers to the dark as the hidden things or the unknown. Our past was permeated with the insecurity of facing the unknown. We had no control over our daily destiny because our fate was determined by those who controlled us. A black mother never knew if she would live to see her children grow. A black family had little hope of spending their years together because their future was unknown. Perhaps one of the most troublesome aspects of our dark past was uncertainty because it created an inability to plan or dream.

Our dark past brought us trials, but the Lord brought us longsuffering. Our dark past brought us criticism, but the Lord gave us contentment. Our dark past brought us strain, but the Lord gave us stability. Our dark past brought us hardships, but the Lord brought us hope. Throughout our history, we have always found a crack somewhere for a little light from heaven to shine through so we could steal away and be in the presence of the Lord. We survived the excruciating circumstances of our past because we held onto the powerful hand of God.

From the recess of our dark past, we have come a mighty long way. Out of our dark past we have come listening to the ragtime of Scott Joplin, the jazz of Satchmo Armstrong, and the syncopated orchestration of Quincy Jones. Out of our dark past we have come to appreciate the baritone of Paul Roberson, the soprano of Marian Anderson and the operatic perfection of Leontyne Price. Out of our dark past we have felt the knock out punches of Jack Johnson, Joe Louis and Mike Tyson. We watched Muhammad Ali float like a butterfly and sting like a bee. Out of our dark past we have run the Olympic tracks with the fleeting feet of Wilma Rudolph, the blazing speed of Jesse Owens and the amazing feats of Michael Johnson. Out of our dark past we have discovered the mysteries of science with George Washington Carver, Daniel Hale Williams and Mark Dean. Out of our dark past we have learned from the great minds of Mary McCloud Bethune, J. S. Clark and Johnetta Cole. Out of our dark past we have come shouting with the great preaching of thundering pulpiteers such as Caesar Clark, William H. Norwood, Perry Simmons, Sr. and C. L. Franklin. Out of our dark past we have marched to the civil rights cadence set by Frederick Douglas, Martin Luther King, Jesse Jackson and Al Sharpton. Out of our dark past, we have sung songs of rejoicing with Roberta Martin, Mahalia Jackson and Lucy Campbell, who told us "There's something within me that holdeth the reins." Out of my past, I heard my late grandmother, Annier Norwood, singing "It's another year and I ain't gone."

We survived our dark past. Now it is time to focus on our future. First John 2:8 compares the life of a Christian and a non-Christian as one who is moving from mediocrity to fulfillment. In the "b" section of verse 8, John tells us: *"The darkness is past, and the true light now shineth."*

If we are to have a bright future, we must bring some good things our foreparents gave us from our past. Firstly, we must bring our faith in God. No matter what we try to do in the future, we must trust God to lead us. Secondly, we should be grateful for what God gives us. Thirdly, we should teach our children to put first things first; that is, education before TV, marriage before babies and home ownership before Cadillacs. Fourthly, we should use ingenuity to make what we need from what we have. Finally, if we are to have a bright future, we must rebuild the moral and spirtual foundations of our homes and our churches. We must return to calling right right and wrong wrong.

The Lord has brought us from slavery to freedom; from old houses with dirt floors to wall-to-wall carpeting; from kerosene lanterns to electric light; from pot-belly stoves to central heat; from those old cardboard fans to central air; from picking beans to making FUBU jeans; from cutting pulpwood to Hollywood. Yes, the Lord has brought us a mighty long way. Yet, my question remains…

Black man, where art thou?

About the Author

— Rev. Dr. Perry Simmons, Jr. —

Rev. Dr. Perry Simmons, Jr. was born in Cairo, Georgia to the late Rev. Perry Simmons, Sr. and Pinkie Norwood Simmons. He is the fourth of eleven children. He graduated with honors from Washington High School in 1965. He received a Bachelor of Arts from Morris Brown College, Atlanta, Georgia; a Master of Theology from the Interdenominational Theological Center, Atlanta, Georgia; a Master of Arts in Pastoral Ministry from Caldwell College, Caldwell, New Jersey; and a Doctorate of Divinity from Faith College and Seminary, Birmingham, Alabama.

In 1966, he was called to the gospel ministry and, in 1973, began his pastorate at Union Baptist Church in Moultrie, Georgia. He also pastored Macedonia Baptist Church in Valdosta, Georgia; New Mount Pleasant Baptist Church in Waycross, Georgia; Mount Hope Baptist Church in Quitman, Georgia; and Mount Hope Baptist Church in Hahira, Georgia.

On June 20, 1982, Dr. Simmons was called to the Abyssinian Baptist Church in Newark, New Jersey where he has served for the past twenty-two years. Under his leadership, the church has undergone a million dollar expansion and more than 2,500 new members have been added to the body of Christ.

Dr. Simmons is the founder and director of the Simmons Scholarship and Community Service Corporation that has provided more than $300,000 in scholarships to needy students. He is also the founder and Executive Director of the Newark Adult Youth Drug Prevention Partnership Program, which counsels youth about the dangers of using drugs.

In 1984, Dr. Simmons received the Religious Achievement Award from Morris Brown College National Alumni Association. Dr. Simmons was voted Who's Who in Religion in America in 1992. The county of Essex has designated October 27 as "Reverend Dr. Perry Simmons, Jr. Day." In April 2004, he was inducted into the Theta Alpha Kappa National Honor Society for Religious Studies and Theology (Gamma Chapter). He is Moderator of the Christian Fellowship Missionary Baptist Association and vice president of the General Baptist Convention of New Jersey. God willing, he will become president in October 2004.

Dr. Simmons is married to the former Emma Pinckney. He is a proud father and grandfather.